michigan w...... ....

2025 fiction contest

Superior Stories
Helen Raica-Klotz

Michigan Writers Cooperative Press
P. O. Box 2355
Traverse City, Michigan 49685

ISBN-13: 978-1-950744-26-8

Book design by Amy Hansen

The cover features the Portage Lake Lift Bridge, which connects Hancock and Houghton in Michigan's Keweenaw Pensinsula.

Contents

I. Drowning

II. Weather

This book is dedicated to my family and friends
who grew up with me in the Keweenaw.

SUPERIOR STORIES

I. DROWNING

The Canal

Lake Superior is the heavy-weight boxer of the Great Lakes. It weaves behind the tree line; it ducks just beyond the two-lane roads; it jabs its way through the rivers and streams; it pounds the rocky shoreline with relentless force. Here, the big lake stretches into the horizon, no land in sight. There's only water and skyline in the far distance, blues and greys blending into one another like a child's muddy watercolor.

Michigan's Keweenaw Peninsula, the state's northernmost section, sticks out 150 miles into Lake Superior. It's the peninsula on the peninsula, this strip of land and rock. Almost two hundred years ago, copper mining companies and the U.S. government decided to dredge an ambling river used by natives for fishing, expanding it to reach the east and west sides of the lake. This man-made Portage Canal became a sharp forty-mile line, slicing the peninsula cleanly in half. The upper part of the Keweenaw is not a peninsula at all. It is an island.

The streets of Houghton, on the mainland side, and Hancock, on the island side, tumble towards the canal. Businesses and houses cling to the surrounding hills, clustering together near the bridge that links the two towns and small villages beyond. A bit farther south, Michigan Tech glitters at the water's edge. Portage and Torch Lakes connect to the canal from the north, making up the rest of what people call The Keweenaw Waterway. Keweenaw is an Ojibway word for "the crossing place."

****

HELEN RAICA-KLOTZ

Kurt glances up when the door opens. Sunlight cuts through smoky dark air, hovers for a split second above the stained four-tops, the pool table with one pocket held together by duct tape, and the brown linoleum floor. The door slams shut, and the Michelob sign shudders against a paneled wall. Kurt squints. He makes out a Carhart jacket and stained Green Bay Packers hat. Billy. Again. Kurt fixes a smile on his face and pulls a Budweiser from the cooler.

"Hey, man. Long time, no see."

"Yeah, long-time, no see," Billy replies, hefting himself on the barstool. He grabs the beer. "Thanks. Say, when are you going to get that sign fixed? The 'Loading One'? How much does it cost to replace a 'Z,' man?"

"Who knows? I don't own the place. So what's up?"

"Caught two walleye yesterday. Pretty good size. But the ice is getting thin. I'm gonna need to pull the shanty. Hate to give it up—a good place to get away from the old lady, eh?"

Kurt shrugs, trying to stretch his smile a little wider. He watches Billy lift the bottle and take one swig, then another. It's going to be a long Tuesday afternoon.

"Hey," Billy asks. "How's your mom?"

"About the same."

"Yeah, Alzheimer's. It's a bitch. You're a good guy, taking care of her like you do."

Kurt looks down at the sticky floor underneath his feet. Technically, it's dementia. Either way, he ends up introducing himself to his mom every morning before sitting her in front of the television to watch *Price is Right* and *Wheel of Fortune*, a TV tray with Velveeta cheese, Triscuits, and a glass of 7 Up by her side. On good days, she remembers to eat. Every evening, he listens to the same stories about growing up on the farm in Ahmeek, her voice rising and falling the identical way each time, like a record on repeat. He leans against the back of the bar. "Have you heard that Cheryl is back in town?"

"Yup, I heard. Up from Florida, visiting her folks. But I haven't seen her." Billy weaves his head back and forth. "Remember when we were in high school? We would go toke behind the bus barn and then head into the girls' basketball game. Man, Cheryl. She was something to watch. The way those tits bounced in that top and her round little ass in those shorts—oh, and the legs on that one. She could play too. Nice jump shot. Of course, she didn't give me the time of day. All wrapped up in you-know-who."

"Yeah." Kurt struggles to remember most of the girls from high school clearly. Trying to remember back then is like trying to see fish below the water's shifting surface; you know they are down there, but move so quickly, they are almost impossible to see. That was about the time his mom's memory started to go, and it seemed to have taken his memories too. At least, some of them. But it was hard to forget Cheryl—and her husband.

"You know, I never understood what she saw in him. I mean, sure, he was smart. He was supposed to go to Tech. He got that full ride, remember? But he was stupid enough to knock her up, and, well, shit. He ended up selling auto parts at the shop in Hancock. So much for the cushy engineering job and rich life. That's probably why she was with him in the first place. I mean, the minute I get in the door, the old gal is on me for my wallet, especially on payday. Which is why I'm here—gotta spend it before she gets it, you know?"

"Yeah, I guess."

Billy fixes his eyes on the mirror above the taps. Kurt knows the mirror is filthy, its edges littered with old photos, unpaid tabs, a rosary, and some kid's muddy drawing of a dinosaur or maybe a kitten. He waits. He knows what's coming next.

"After Cheryl popped out that second kid, that's when he started showing up here regular," Billy continues. "He would sit at the end of the bar, right over there. Those thick black glasses sliding down his nose, beer perched on his skinny leg, looking around the place like he was new here—just checking it out for the first time.

HELEN RAICA-KLOTZ

Jesus. I always felt like he was studying us low-lifes, like he was so much better than all the rest of us. Since he was here every night, you think he'd figure out that he was one of us after all."

"Right."

"He was a good drunk. I'll give you that. He did it enough to be good at it, eh? He would just drink and drink until you turned off the lights, then stagger to his car and drive the three blocks home. I followed him a couple of times—well, just to make sure he made it. And every time, I would see Cheryl in the window, her hair down around her back, wearing a fuzzy blue bathrobe. He would shuffle in the front door, and she'd disappear. Run to him, I suppose. I tell you, if it were me coming in the door drunk as a skunk, there'd be yelling and screaming. This bastard, though, nothing. The lights would go off, and that would be that. Like, show's over and the movie's done. Grab your empty popcorn carton and leave."

Kurt sighs. He hears the traffic outside. Where's everyone going? Somewhere, he decides. Somewhere else. He picks up his phone, opens iTunes. Bob Seger starts running against the wind. He studies the almost invisible seam in the middle of the bar top, the place where two pieces of large green tile meet to cut a clean line down the center. He runs his thumb against the line, up and then down again, feeling the dull edge of the silence ebb between them. "You know, man, I feel bad about that whole thing."

"I don't," Billy says, shaking his head, left then right. "I mean, what for? We did take him home that weekend, remember? He just passed out, fell off that bar stool, and bam."

"Yeah. Concussion, probably," says Kurt. He picks up a rag and begins wiping an invisible stain on the bar.

"But we picked him up and dragged him into your Chrysler. Man, it was cold that night—like ice in your lungs. We drove him home, and there she was at the door, same hair, in that same fuzzy bathrobe. She reached out, grabbed him, and pulled him inside. Slam. No thank you, no nothing." Billy takes a long drink from his bottle.

"I heard she wanted him to go to the hospital, but he wouldn't go—no insurance. Sad."

"Yup. Sad," Billy agrees.

They go silent. Kurt thinks about taking his duck boat out on the canal soon. He'll bring it out to the west end and drop anchor. The boat's too small to take past the buoys into the big lake. That's fine. He'll just sit there and listen to the waves, the sound of the water pushing him back into town.

Billy puts the empty bottle down, leans forward, and jabs his forefinger on the bar top. "Look, the guy was a drunk. He got drunk. He drove off the road two days later and ended up in the canal. Probably trying to cross the water to get to the next bar. End of story. Concussion or not, it doesn't matter. I'm sure Cheryl's fine now. And those kids were so little, you know, they probably don't even remember him. He's just some picture on the wall, nobody real anymore."

Real. Right. Kurt points at Billy, and Billy nods. Kurt grabs another Bud from the cooler and places the bottle on the bar.

"Thanks. These go down pretty easy, don't they? You know, when they fished him out of the water, I heard he had 300 bucks in his pocket. Probably keeping it from the wife. Maybe he wasn't so stupid after all."

The Sands

The Keweenaw Peninsula is known as "The Copper Country" since it was home to over 150 copper mines and mills from the mid-1800s to the turn of the century. The remains of this industry litter the landscape. Empty mills, with crumbling bricks and broken windows, squat along M-26. A dredge stands in Torch Lake, tilting wildly to its side like a drunken uncle. The Lutheran and Catholic cemeteries are filled with the names of hundreds of miners who were blown up, buried under a landslide, or fell to their deaths in the shafts deep underground.

But the most visible reminder of copper mining is the stamp sand. This black, coarse sand was left from the processing of ore to extract copper. Since many mills were built along the Keweenaw Waterway and sections of Lake Superior, stamp sand was dumped into these lakes. This sand is like crystalized coal, shattered and scattered in a million pieces that cover the shoreline. They say around half of Torch Lake is filled with this sand, which shifts easily with the currents, moving through local rivers and nearby lakes. Stamp sand is considered toxic since it contains trace amounts of heavy metals and leaching chemicals. Fish in these waters are not considered safe to eat. Little to no vegetation can grow on the sand, and without plants or grasses to hold it in place, it spreads through the air on windy days, coating cars, houses, and buildings with fine black dust.

About fifty years ago, U.S. Superfund dollars were used to erect fences around the sands. Native plants were placed throughout the sites and promptly died from the combination of lead and mercury in the soil. Too much to move and impossible to remediate, the stamp sand was eventually covered with topsoil purchased with the remaining government funds. Some houses now sit on these sites, cheap waterfront properties.

****

Paula knows John is there, standing behind her even before she turns around. Funny. She always knows he's there: he has a way of hovering, invading her orbit with his smell, like dying carp. No, not his smell. His neediness. She takes one last look at the long table, filled with half-eaten casseroles, wilting salads, a few bags of Bunny Bread, and a tub of margarine. She straightens her shoulders and turns. "John," she says.

"Paula! I didn't see you standing there. I swear, funerals always make me so hungry. I don't even like macaroni salad, and here I am, piling it on my plate." He smiles, the spit or mayonnaise in the left corner of his mouth stretching upwards. "How are you?"

"Good. But sad, you know? I liked Aunt Priscilla."

Yeah," says John, nodding a little too emphatically. "Our aunt was a good lady. Cancer sucks. I remember when we were kids, she could blow smoke out of her nose; she looked like a Chinese dragon, puffing away. Priscilla, and grandma, and your mom and dad, and mine too—all of them sitting around every summer at the old house, smoking the cigs and shooting the shit, while we ran around the neighborhood."

"Mmm." She takes some dried carrot sticks, browning celery, and a few tomatoes from a veggie tray and moves towards an empty table, sliding into a folding chair wedged against the wall. John slides in beside her. She glances up, hoping someone else will join them.

"Paula. Man. It's been years. We used to spend so much time together."

Paula nods. She concentrates on stabbing a cherry tomato

with her plastic spork. The tomato wobbles, then shoots away on her paper plate.

"We were little savages, don't you remember? In the summer, I would swipe a loaf of bread and a jar of peanut butter from the house, and we would drink out of the garden hose out back if we got thirsty because no one would bother to feed us until dinner. And at night, we would sneak in the back door of Jilbert's Dairy. We'd snitch cartons of chocolate milk, sit on the rotting picnic table in the dark, and see who could belch the loudest. You always won. Wanna try again?" John looks at her expectantly.

She shakes her head once.

"Okay. Just kidding." He sticks his bony elbow into her side hard, making her wince. "Remember, we would dare each other to lay down on the railroad tracks behind the dairy? We had to lay there until one of us saw the train coming around the bend. I can remember this like it was yesterday. The sun in my eyes, the track rattling beneath my head, and that train whistle, so far off and so close at the same time, you know?"

Paula closes her eyes. There is a moment of silence.

"How's your dad doing?" she asks. They both look over at his father. His belly strains over his belt, and his pant legs puddle over his Sorels. He sways slightly over the dessert table, staring at the cookies and brownies in their plastic boxes. Uncle Billy, thinks Paula. Drunk already.

"Oh, he's good. The same as always. Hey, do you remember Barry?"

Paula tries to conjure a person to fit this name, but all she can think of is the TV show with the same title, the one about a hit man who wanted to be an actor.

"Yes, yes, you do." John stabs his own spork in the air, as if to emphasize his description. "He was the guard, the security guy at the Horner Flooring. We would see him most nights when we went to climb the lumber piles. You remember this, don't you? We would climb to the top of the logs. From there, you could see everything: the tarpaper roofs of our houses, the busted snow-mobile in your backyard, the rusty metal swing set in mine, and your dog, Daisy? Always outside, chained to that big tree. In the summer, you could see the lake in the distance, but in the winter, all you could see was white—just piles of snow everywhere. Does any of this ring a bell?"

Of course it rings a bell. Many bells. But that is all in the past. She has a life now, a good job downstate, and even a quasi-boyfriend.

"And remember how you got your boot stuck between the logs one night? It was wedged in there so tight, and you started crying, and I told you to hush up, that we would figure it out. In the end, we left your boot there, and you had to walk home in your cotton sock. Your dad whooped you good for that one. But we were able to get the boot out the next week, after the thaw. It was a purple and red moon boot, and when we pried it from the log, it was soaking wet, but you wore it home that night. It made a squishing sound every time you took a step. Funny, the stuff you remember."

"Funny. So, Barry? You were saying?"

"Right. Barry. He was the guy at the lumberyard. A big guy, he kinda shuffled when he walked, like a bear. He always smelled like sweat and bologna. We used to hide from him until he found us and invited us into his warming hut. Most nights, we would go and huddle by the electric heater. Sometimes, he'd even pour us some coffee from his plaid thermos. Sheesh, he could have been a child molester, right? But he wasn't. He was just Barry."

Paula does not remember this, but she nods again and looks down. Food is still on her plate, but she can't eat anymore. "I've got to get going."

"Okay. But hey, you've got to remember swimming in the canal in the summertime. The black sand? It was always so hot, like walking on charcoal. We would race to see who could get to the water first, the soles of our feet on fire, and we would dare each other to be the first to go under. Then we would swim past that downed oak tree, out into the middle of the canal where the bottom was all black, and you couldn't see anything. Hey, do you remember a kid drown there?"

This, Paula remembers. She remembers the boy, standing in the water all by himself. His pale belly pushes out over the top of his cut-off denim shorts, his arms and legs are thick and flabby, and long hair blows in his face like spent ragweed. Paula can still feel the soft, playdough flesh of his back beneath her palms. There is the hard shove, the brilliantly loud splash of water, the shrieks of laughter. When she looks back, she sees him on his hands and knees, his stringy hair plastered to his scalp. She still sees his eyes, clear and blue, watching her as she swims out to join her friends. And later, when she comes back to shore, she sees the crowd huddled on the black sand, the red and white lights of the police car playing over the dark water's surface.

"I remember something like that," Paula says, standing up.

"Oh, yeah," John nods again. "They found his body washed up on the rocks by the college. Some Tech student found him. They said he was all white and bloated, and his eyes had been eaten out by the fish. He wasn't a down stater. He was somebody local. Hakala? Hiltunen? He lived out past Houghton somewhere. It was in the papers and everything. Hey, weren't you and your friends out there the day it happened? Crazy. I mean, ten years old. Who leaves a kid alone like that?"

The Bridge

I n the Keweenaw, the Portage Bridge straddles the Portage Canal, the only link between the mainland and the island. The bridge's two lift towers bracket the sky, the cables strung loosely between like a sagging clothesline. White with a blue underbelly, the bridge seems to float above the water in summer. In winter, the lights atop the towers shimmer against the ice and snow below.

The bridge has two large decks, its lower deck designed to lift 100 feet in the air to make way for large boats to pass underneath. When the bridge is lifted, all traffic stops: cars line roads on either side, snaking around hills, waiting for the bridge to drop. Typically, however, the lower deck is raised to street level, about 30 feet above the water, allowing smaller boats to pass without moving the bridge at all. In winter, the lower deck hovers five feet from the waterline. Snowmobiles cross over on the lower deck, and automobiles use the upper deck, until ice and snow melt away from the canal. Built in the 1950s, it is the heaviest and widest lift bridge in the United States.

In recent years, the bridge has been the site of protests, about almost everything: the lack of funding for high school sports, the Black Lives Matter movement, the 2020 election, Abortion Rights and Right to Life. It is the most visible location for sharing opinions. People stand on the narrow bike lane, waving hand-printed cardboard signs and shouting slogans as cars rumble past. Injustices are aired here, something the builders never imagined. The bridge was, after all, simply a way to cross the water to the other side.

****

HELEN RAICA-KLOTZ

The kitchen is a mess. Cheerios stuck like ticks on the side of the bowls, milk slopped over the counter, the bottom of the coffee pot giving off its acrid, burnt smell. You would think the kids could rinse their bowls or at least turn off the coffee pot. Cheryl notices a paper on the table, tattooed with oversized hearts and a few half-finished algebra problems. She picks it up, sighs, and puts it back down. She starts to run water in the sink, grabs a curled sponge. She can feel exhaustion behind her eyes, grainy and dark. If she gets this done, she can get a good seven hours of sleep before school gets out. Her phone vibrates in her back pocket. She pulls it out and takes a deep breath. Susan.

"Hey there!"

"Hey, girl! I thought I'd give you a call, see what's up."

"Not much," says Cheryl, putting the phone on speaker, placing it next to the dying aloe plant on the windowsill. She stacks more dishes in the water. "Looking forward to seeing you."

"Oh, yeah. I am so looking forward to it. Four weeks and we'll be sitting by your pool, drinking margaritas in the sunshine! I can't wait. You are so lucky you moved down to Florida and got out of this godforsaken winter."

"Yeah, lucky," says Cheryl. She notices the Ritalin bottle on the windowsill is almost empty. Time to get that refilled. And make the appointment with the dentist, throw in load of laundry, write the check for spring soccer—and hope the check doesn't bounce.

"I was telling Derek, we have got to get new tires on the Fiesta. The other day, I was going down the hill and the back end started to shimmy around. I almost did a 360. I downshifted, but it doesn't matter much if you're skating on sheer ice. Thank God for that intersection on Eighth Street, where it flattens out. Every time I go to work, I feel like I'm on that nasty carnival ride—the tilt-a-whirl? The one that made you throw up every time. Seriously, I thought I was going to end up in the canal."

"Wow. That's crazy." Cheryl finishes the dishes and moves

on to the table. Is that ketchup, that red jellied mass? She tries scraping it with her thumbnail. It doesn't budge.

"God," Susan sighs. "Yesterday was a day." There is a pause, and Cheryl knows what her friend wants her to say. She slumps down on a kitchen stool and glances at the clock. 8:14 am.

"What happened?"

"I saw her again—you know, the client I was telling you about? The one that moved up here last year, after the..." here Susan pauses, "incident? She came in, sat down, hunched over in the chair, and started pulling on her bangs. She pulls until the hair comes right out. I don't think she even knows she's doing it. When she took off her coat, she looked so thin. And her eyes are, well, she looks terrible. She just sits there, staring down her boots making pools of dirty water on that awful gray carpet. I really need to get a new rug in there, something to cheer up the place. Maybe I can stop at Walmart this weekend and find something."

Cheryl doesn't want to know, but at the same time, she does. "Is she doing any better?"

"Nope. The same. She says, 'I remember how he screamed so loud when he was born. I remember the birthmark on his back that was shaped like a lopsided heart. I remember his second birthday party where he ate so much chocolate cake and drank so much Coke that he threw up that night, and the vomit was all brown and sticky.' Seriously. She remembers how he would suck his right thumb, then his left thumb, how he laughed so loud when he finally figured out how to make his Big Wheel work, and how he went to sleep with his Barney, you know, that purple dinosaur on TV? She says she would sing him that song, 'I love you, you love me' every night. Well, probably not every night, but that's what she says."

Cheryl feels her heart clench. She imagines the blood freezing, turning to ice in her veins. God, she was tired. "Have you asked her how she's doing, like, now?"

"Well, of course I ask her how she is doing now. That's my job, right? But she just shakes her head and stops talking. Seriously, all she wants to do is talk about him before, you know. I can't get her to move on. Six months of this. I don't know what I'm supposed to do. These are the days I hate my job."

"Yeah, I get it." Cheryl takes another deep breath. She looks out the kitchen window. The sun is reflecting off grey aluminum siding of the trailer next door. The light is sharp, too harsh. Her gaze moves to hover on the cobweb in the corner of the sill, a dead fly hanging in the center. She looks away. "Hey, listen, I got to go. I'm coming off another third shift, and if I don't get to sleep soon, I swear I'm going to be a walking zombie."

"Well, okay. I understand." Susan pauses. Cheryl pauses too. The line of silence stretches out, taut between them. "So, I gotta tell you. There was one day she came in, maybe a couple months ago, that I didn't tell you about. It was the day the hot water heater went out, remember? And Derek stayed home to get the part, the new thermostat, and I went in to work late. God, I felt awful that day: my hair was so greasy, and I swear I stunk, even though I put on a ton of deodorant. So, that day she came in, eyes all glassy, reeking of pot. She was stoned—not a good combination with all the meds she's on. She sort of stumbled in and headed straight to the window. She pulled open the plastic blinds to look at the water. Then she put her face to the glass, her breath making it fog up. When I asked how she was doing, she was quiet for the longest time, just standing there, her and that foggy window, looking at the canal, the bridge, all the cars. Then she said, 'Do you know what a dead baby feels like when you hold him?'"

"Oh, Christ."

"I know. Thank God I have training. So I said, like I was taught to do, 'No. Do you want to tell me?' I really didn't want to hear, but she needed to say it, you know?"

Yes, Cheryl thought. She knew.

"She said when he was born, it was like a bridge appeared out of nowhere. She walked across, and she was in this different world—one that was bright, like summer all the time. She was able to feel, to really feel things. 'I was a real person there,' she said. But then her baby drowned, an accident, you know, he wandered off when they were at the park by the canal. The lifeguard pulled him out, but it was too late. She said when she held him, his lips were gray, his blue swim trunks were stuck to his little legs, but his eyes were wide open. She said she can still see him, still feel the weight of his body in her arms. But she can't feel anything else, not anymore. Nothing."

For a split second, Cheryl wishes she were this woman, unable to feel anything: no fear, no anger, no exhaustion. And no kids. No more being suspended between you and them. Just a sharp, clear line down the middle, with you and your own life on the other side. She stands up abruptly and shakes her head. "So sad."

"I know, right? I didn't even get a chance to say anything. She just turned around and left the office. I stood there, staring at the fog on the window until it disappeared. Then I closed the blinds. I was worried, but she came back the next week, and the week after that, and now we just talk about what she remembers. I guess that's okay. Everyone deals with grief differently."

"Yeah, we all do. That's for sure."

"So, anyways. Tires for the car and a new carpet. I'll talk to Derek tonight. I swear to you, I don't want to end up in that canal. I've got a trip to take soon, right? Hey, how was your day?"

II. WEATHER

Hoar Frost

Hoar frost is rare, even in the Keweenaw Peninsula of Michigan. It requires a cold, clear, utterly still night, one with low humidity and just the right temperature. Then it happens. Overnight, all remaining water in the air freezes, and by morning, the entire world is covered in frail, delicate ice crystals. Like spun sugar, a confectioner's dream, these spirals of frost blanket everything: tall grasses and barbed wire fences, maple leaves and kitchen windows, milkweed stalks and car rooftops. It is magical. Because there is no wind, nothing moves; everything is frozen in time, silver-white and glittering. This frost is so light it usually disappears by noon. The sun melts the apparition as if it was never there.

****

Trisha had a crush on Jesus. He was hot. Seventeen different versions of his portrait, torn from the cover of the First Lutheran Church's Sunday bulletin, were scotch-taped to her bedroom wall. Some of these were headshots, featuring his soft dark eyes, full lips, and long hair. Some were full body, featuring Our Savior in his flowing robes and brown sandals, looking benevolently at a sheep or calf cradled in his arms. Trisha would stare at these pictures. She had no pictures of him pinned to the cross, emaciated and bleeding. That was gross. But during Sunday School, she would find herself looking past Pastor Neimi, a pale, pimply faced man with hair the color of rotting potatoes, to the altar where Jesus was hung. The Son of God was pinned to the back wall like a butterfly. She would studiously avoid the bleeding hands and feet,

HELEN RAICA-KLOTZ

the crown of thorns piercing his temple, and instead fix her gaze on the drape of fabric folded just so over his pelvis.

Trisha's mother, a high school English teacher, had decorated Trisha's room years ago when she was pregnant and hopeful. She had hung pink floral wallpaper, but now, the grooves of the cheap paneling underneath were visible, and the paper had begun to peel by the ceiling. A trundle bed was wedged under the window, next to a battered pine dresser and a wicker desk reclaimed from the teacher's lounge. The desk was repainted white, words and numbers like hieroglyphics etched into the surface, one on top of the other, a desperate attempt to find meaning from hours of homework. Trisha lives at this desk. Here, she drinks Tang, paints her fingernails pink, and practices her flute, trying to chase the sixteenth notes that spiral to the end of "Windy." And all the while, the seventeen Jesuses look down with love in their eyes.

She is sitting at the wicker desk today, books and papers pushed to one side. Trisha can see the top of her head in the mirror that hangs above the desk. Her part is slightly askew. The surface of the desk is bordered by woven wicker. Trisha traces the pattern of the weave with her eyes. She hears the clock in the hallway. She breathes in and out. The wicker curves. The clock ticks. All that matters is her capacity to sit, immobile, in that space. Time beats its tiny wings against her face, and she doesn't even flinch.

She is thinking of Mr. Cohen again. He, too, has dark hair, dark eyes. The first day of band class, he looked directly at her, sitting quietly, flute in her lap, back straight. Jon banged the snare drum out of time, Vicki doodled pictures of fairies and flowers in her clarinet music, and Janet and Lisa whispered behind her. But she didn't care. She watched Mr. Cohen, who stood at the podium above her. She was close enough to see where his mustache was coming in, a faint smudge above his lips, and the way his hair curled elegantly around his left ear.

How's the new band teacher?" her mother asked, steering their rusted Pinto out of the gravel parking lot that afternoon. Trisha nodded, looking out the window. She wondered which car was his. "I hear the seniors ate him alive. Be good to him, okay? It's hard to be a long-term sub, especially a young one. That poor kid. He's never even been in the U.P. before."

Yes, Trisha thought. That is why his thin pale hands were shaking as he tried beating time with his baton. He would begin to move his arms, waving them over to the melody. She could almost hear it, notes bright and clear in the distance. She could tell Mr. Cohen heard it too. But then Vicki's clarinet squeaked, the entire row burst into laughter, and the room descended into chaos. "He looks like he's drowning," Janet whispered. Lisa giggled.

The next week, while her mother graded poorly written freshman essays after school, Trisha wandered into the band room. Mr. Cohen stood before the blackboard etched with music staffs, chalk in hand, puzzling out a series of indecipherable notes. He turned to see her. He smiled, a flickering lightbulb, and stood up straighter. "Hello, Trisha. How can I help you?" She told him she wanted some help with her flute, to get the trill down for the upcoming concert. "I want to be better," she said. He looked at her for a moment. "Okay." They agreed to meet Wednesday afternoons after school, and she arrived every Wednesday to find him there. Sometimes, he would be seated at the battered upright piano, pouring over pages of music thick with black notes. Sometimes, he would be staring out the window. His smile started to stay on, not flicker out. He would tell her stories as she held her flute to her face, the cool metal shaft against her cheek.

"Teacher's pet," Janet said as they left band class one day. "More like teacher's whore," Lisa said. She ignored them. Her mother told her not to listen to fools, to work hard, and to go to college. "Things will be different there," she promised. Trisha envisioned the ivy-covered buildings circling a large lawn dappled with sunshine. Here, she would sit underneath an oak tree on a large plaid blanket, books and friends piled up on either side.

But when she asked Mr. Cohen about college, he said flatly, "It's alright."

Instead, he told her about kayaking down the Tobacco River, the trees awash with reds and golds, the shock of blue against the curve of the sand up at Eagle Harbor, and the sound of pine trees groaning in the wind behind his rental in Hubbell. One day he told her he went to Jacobs Falls. "I heard that in the middle of winter, ice makes a platform over the top of the falls, so you can stand way out there, watching the water crash underneath your feet. I'd love to see this."

She nodded. She had never been to any of these places only miles from her house. But she loved the sound of his voice, sweet and dark like a Hershey's bar, each story a little rectangle of sweetness she would hold on her tongue. She sat utterly still and listened.

She talked to him too, about the blue jay that flew into the window during biology class, her love of *A Tree Grows in Brooklyn*, and her dream of living in a big city. Mostly, she told him stories of what she does know of this place, which he seemed to like. She talked of the way snow piles up outside of the kitchen window in winter, how blackflies swarm the beach in summer, and how ragweed and sweet pea spill into the gully behind her house in spring. He listened to these stories with such intensity. She felt a glow in her chest every time she left the room. It was divine.

One day, Mr. Cohen said she should consider playing the French horn. "My instrument. You have the right embouchure for it. Besides, colleges are always looking for French horn players. There might be a scholarship there. Who knows?"

He brought his horn for her the next day, lifting the instrument from its shiny velvet case. The keys were like miniature piano pedals, the pipes knitted together in a whirl that flared out at one end. "Here, try," he said, placing the horn in her lap. It felt right and wrong at the same time, like a brass child curled on her legs. Mr. Cohen placed one of her hands on the flat keys and tucked the other deep inside the horn's curved opening. The instrument pressed into her pelvis.

"You play like this," he said. "And the embouchure, it's like a kiss. Pucker your lips together, and blow through the small hole." He turned to her. She looked at his mouth. His lips were slightly chapped. They were scrunched up towards her. She closed her eyes, pushed her lips out as far as she could, and leaned towards him.

She hadn't known that silence could have its own sound. At first, it hummed a faint tremolo, then it ran down the scale until it hung in the air, heavy and dark.

She heard the shriek of the metal chair legs against the battered wood floor. She opened her eyes. He stood quickly. "I gotta go. An appointment," his voice rose on the last word as if it were a question.

She protested. At least, she thought she did, but before she knew it, he had grabbed his parka and backpack and left. She looked down at the horn, tracing its spirals with her eyes, around and down and around again. It wasn't until her mother arrived in the doorway, anxious to get home and start dinner, that she put the instrument back into the case and closed it.

Now Mr. Cohen looks different. His eyes are glassy, pupils impossibly large, like the dead deer splayed out on Highway Two. She can smell the Tic Tacs he crunches between his teeth from her first-row seat. And he never sees her, not really. "Man, Mr. C. is stoned today," Jon snorted on the way out of class. "He's stoned every day," said Lisa. When Trisha stops by after school, the band room door is locked.

This afternoon, her mother told her that Mr. Cohen will be leaving at the end of this week to head back down state since Mrs. Heikkinen's maternity leave is over. "You need to return that French horn. You never play it anyway." Trisha watched her mother scrape the ice condensed on the inside of the windshield with her Visa card. The defroster was on the fritz again. The tiny

HELEN RAICA-KLOTZ

window to the world grew large, then smaller and smaller again as they drove home.

Trisha lifts her eyes to the pictures of her seventeen Jesuses on the wall. They regard her silently. Their eyes are slightly narrowed, their lips a thin line of disappointment. She shakes her head hard, once, twice, and then again. When she opens her eyes, their faces are blurred, out of focus. She stands up. She wedges her fingers behind a picture of Jesus and a lamb. She pulls. He rips in half, his sandals and legs still stuck to the wall. She pulls the Jesuses off, one by one, crumbling their faces, their bodies, and letting them fall to the floor. When she is finished, all she can see are the pink pale roses curving up her wall, like Jesus was never there.

Lake Effect Snow

I n the Keweenaw, lake effect snow is caused by cold arctic air sweeping down over Lake Superior, picking up moisture as it heads toward land. Charcoal clouds billow over the big lake. The surface of the water and shoreline turn a mottled gray, a pencil sketch without color, until the white flakes start to fall, light and feathery, like powdered sugar swirling from the sky. Because of its unique geography, the Keweenaw is one of the snowiest regions in the United States east of the Rockies. The conditions are perfect. In winter, the snow often lasts days at a time, constant and relentless. It becomes a child's snow globe, one that gets shaken again and again. Soon everything is covered in heaping mounds of white, leaving only the vaguest outline of what lies underneath.

****

"Conditions are perfect," his dad says. Tommy knows it. He watched the storm sweep across the western half of the U.P. this morning, his phone screen filled with swatches of swirling white and blue.

"Ten inches by tomorrow, all packed and groomed and ready to go. You should come up, buddy, and ski with the old man." He tries to sound light, but the plea underneath is audible. The last time Tommy saw him, he looked so old: shirt hanging off his thin shoulders, gray hair sticking out in clumps underneath his Carhart cap, a sloppy shave leaving bristles jutting out from his pale chin. That heart attack really did a number on him.

"Yup, sounds good, Dad. I'll try and get up on Saturday. We

can hit the hill by noon, okay?" And it did sound good: to get over to Powderhorn, ski some real runs. "I'll talk to Tina tonight." Tommy ignores the way his own chest constricts at these words. "Gotta go, Dad. Love ya."

He pulls into the back of Mt. Ripley's parking lot on the way home. He gets out of his battered Subaru, lights a blunt, and leans back on his car hood. It is Monday night, so the hill is empty. The floodlights glitter off the fresh powder, and the Red Lift stitches way up the face, the chairs seesawing in the wind. His dad taught him to ski here as a kid. On winter weekends, they would be up at 7:30 to be out for first turns. His dad would head for the black diamonds, schussing his way over the neat corduroy lines of snow that lead down to the lodge. But Tommy loved skiing the ungroomed side trails. He would head to the back of the mountain and carve his way through the deep snow, working to lift his skis above the drifts. The snow would billow around him when he turned, making it almost impossible to see. Tommy had to feel his way down, skimming past outstretched pines and hidden rocks. It was a rush.

He takes one final toke and looks up. The soft flakes have begun their dance through the sky. Time to go. The engine starts on the third try, and the headlights cut two tracks through falling snow.

When he arrives home, Tina and Sam are curled together on the La-Z-Boy, and Gracie is still in her pajamas. "She refused to get dressed," Tina says. It doesn't really matter. The thermostat is set at 76 degrees, and the windows are fogged with the heat. Tommy bends to kiss her and the baby. Sam dozes in a tangle of blankets, one arm splayed over his head. "Daddy!" Gracie shrieks and wraps her chubby arms around Tommy's legs. She looks up. "Gonna get'cho?" She smiles and runs, skirting the Formica table and cat food bowls.

"Oh, yeah—the tickle monster is going to get you," Tommy says, chasing her down the narrow hallway. They end up in a pile on her bed. Tommy grabs her belly. She shrieks in delight.

"You've trained her to do that, you know," Tina says, but Tommy can hear the smile in her voice. "Only daddy can be the tickle monster."

"That's right. My little Pavlovian dog. Ruff, Gracie." Tommy growls, and she giggles.

"Doggie daddy," she says and runs back down the hallway. Tommy lays on her bed, tracing the pink roses of the wallpaper with his eyes. Another strip near the ceiling is starting to come loose, revealing the brown paneling underneath. "Daddy?"

Tommy heads into the kitchen, pulling out a box of mac and cheese from the cupboard, wilted lettuce and a half a tomato from the fridge. He moves the breakfast dishes into the sink, sodden circles of Fruit Loops swimming in blue milk. "Did you eat today?" he asks Tina.

"Mmm, a bit," she replies. She turns, and Tommy watches her. Tina is losing weight as Sam gains it, often forgetting to have lunch if Tommy is not around to remind her. When she bends over, Tommy can see the bones of her spine and ribcage jutting through her shirt.

Gracie and Tommy eat dinner. Tina moves the food around her plate. Sam's head raises from Tina's chest. He starts to squall, a low rumble that gains intensity as his body twists and contorts in Tina's lap. She gets up and walks with the baby into the living room. Gracie sings about the itsy, bitsy spider who falls down with old McDonald on his farm. One of the red barrettes in her hair has come loose, dangling over her plate as she rocks back and forth. Tina returns to the table. Sam's mouth is firmly latched to her breast, his eyes closed again.

Tommy talks about work. He tells Tina about the couple that came in to buy a sofa, tried to get conditional approval for the store loan, but got turned down after the credit check. This happens a lot. It's a bummer. They really could have used the commission. Then it's bath, books, and bedtime for Gracie. The routine never varies. When his former high school English teacher decided to move to Florida, she said she wasn't ready to sell her house and offered to rent it to Tommy. They were lucky, he knew, to have this place. But some nights, with the smell of cat litter and dirty diapers that Tina's scented candles can't mask, Tommy feels like he's being buried alive. On those nights, he lies in bed, his entire body rigid, stiff, unyielding.

After Gracie is asleep, Tommy and Tina sit on the couch. Tommy clicks on the TV. Sam is still pinned to her chest. "Do you want me to hold him for a while?"

"No. He just fell asleep again. I'm good." Tina's head is tilted towards Sam's face, and Tommy can see that she hasn't washed her hair in a while. Her part is greasy and thick.

"Dad called today," Tommy says. He fixes his eyes on the screen, a commercial for a Ford pickup making its way up the side of an icy hill. Tina says nothing. "He says there's good snow up there right now. He asked me to come up and ski with him. You know, he can't really go by himself, not with his heart and everything. I'm thinking I'd go up on Saturday, just for the day." Tommy waits. Silence. The truck finishes its climb. The ad is over.

Tommy glances at Tina. Sam has woken up. He raises his head. His eyes are open, glazed over. A milky white cloud hovers over the sky of his blue eyes. He looks out, but he sees nothing. He'll never see anything. Blind at birth. A genetic condition, they were told.

"Whatever you want," Tina says. She gets up and takes Sam into the bedroom, shutting the door behind her.

Tommy leans back on the couch. He remembers the last time he was on Powderhorn, the end of the season last year. A blizzard. The wind picked up suddenly when he was on the lift, the chair swinging wildly from side to side like an out-of-control pendulum. By the time he reached the top of the mountain, the snow had turned to hard pellets, ricocheting off his jacket and helmet. He knew there were other people up there, that the bottom of the hill was just eight or nine turns down. But he couldn't see it, any of it.

Tommy froze. It took everything he had to reach down, snap out of his skis, and start down the steep slope, his heavy boots sliding out from underneath him as he fumbled his way slowly down the run. Later, in the warmth of the lodge, his shaky fingers wrapped around a Budweiser, he smiled and told his dad that you just can't predict the weather. But it wasn't the weather. It was him.

Tommy looks out the window, watching the snow starting to cling to the broken screen. He will give his dad a call tomorrow and explain. Conditions weren't quite right after all.

HELEN RAICA-KLOTZ

Black Ice

Black ice typically occurs during the spring thaw in the Keweenaw, when the snow melts and refreezes. Because it lacks air bubbles, this ice is difficult to see. On land, roads and sidewalks are coated with a thin sheen of frozen water, smooth and slick as glass. Road salt becomes ineffective when the sun goes down and the temperature plummets. The ice makes it dangerous to drive and difficult to walk. Near the edges of inland lakes and the Portage Canal, black ice is a misnomer. Here the ice is blue, thin enough to see the water underneath. Only the drunk or stupid venture out too far. Fault lines form and spiderweb across the surface. When the ice finally breaks in spring, it cracks as it splinters and shatters, pieces of a puzzle that can never be put together again.

****

The Rolling Stones, again. Jake sighs. On Muzak. Like, the worst. Who wants to listen to "Time on My Side" played that slowly on a cello? The heavy wooden door slides open, and Jake stretches a smile across his face like Saran Wrap. A man steps into the lobby, moving deftly past the emerald couch and glass table arranged by the large windows. Not bad looking. Nice cheekbones, good haircut, expensive parka. But his slim body is folded forward ever so slightly, eyes fixed on the marble floor under his feet.

"Welcome to the Vault Hotel," Jake says. "How can I help you?"

"Hello," the man replies, raising his eyes to meet Jake's face. "I am checking in for two nights, under the name David Paul." Jake studies his eyes, dark and shiny, pupils almost indistinguishable.

What kind of name is David Paul for this guy? Jake turns to the computer screen.

"Yes, Mr. Paul. I have you here for two nights in the Found Money Suite, on the third floor, room 315." A rich Asian. Of course. He totally belongs in this place, the old Houghton National Bank turned into an upscale hotel for bougie tourists. Rooms named after money, for those with money. Mr. Paul turns to his wallet, and Jake studies him again. It's not the eyes that bug him; that's racist shit. No, it's the meekness of the man, like he's apologizing with his entire body. I mean, nowadays, he should be flaunting he's Oriental, not hiding it behind some American name, Midwest accent, and a North Face jacket.

Jake hands over the keycard, explains concierge service, and validates the parking pass. Mr. Paul offers his thanks and moves smoothly toward the elevator, pulling his compact suitcase behind him, the wheels clicking faintly on the glossy white floor.

He's like a miscast actor—dressed like Ryan Gosling, looks like Jackie Chan. Jake will have to share that one with Terrance tonight. He can see him now, Terrance, with his wine glass propped on the balcony railing of his two-bedroom condo, looking out at the canal. He likes to stand there at night after work, legs spread like he's the captain of the ship ready to set sail. He will tip his head back, laughter spilling out in the cold winter air, his pale skin catching the evening light, his soft blond curls framing his skull. Damn. Terrance. One good-looking dude.

Jake couldn't believe his luck. His last real boyfriend was cute too but a total asshole, their entire relationship so secret even the guy's girlfriend hadn't known about it. At least, Jake didn't think she knew, until one morning he woke up to "Faggot" spraypainted on the windshield of his pickup truck. They broke up pretty quickly after that. Jake still sees him around town. He works as cook at Suomi Bakery, saddled with a kid and growing a potbelly. Jake was lucky he and Terrance had patched things up after last month. It was Jake's own fault, really. He had been on the phone with his cousin downstate, forgetting about the lasagna until the smoke alarm went off. Terrance came home to find smoke billowing around the condo, Jake frantically trying to open all the windows. He was hoping he might be able to hide his mistake, meet Terrance in the hallway and cajole him for a dinner out: no harm, no foul. Except it didn't work that way. The next day, Jake found himself with a sizable black eye and his belongings in two black garbage bags outside the door. Terrance was gone.

That was a rough week. He left the condo and moved into the crappy duplex on Eighth with his sister and her husband, the Lutheran minister. He slept in the guest room with the large crucifix on the wall. A few times, his brother-in-law came in to talk to him, turning his acne-scarred face towards Jake, eyes filled with pity. "Jesus said, 'I tell you, Peter, before the rooster crows, you will betray me three times,'" he read from the worn Bible balanced on his lap. "But Jesus forgave him. Jesus forgives all sins, if you simply ask." Jake fought the urge to roll his eyes. Instead, he adopted an earnest expression and nodded politely, listening to the old alarm clock slide its digits, minute into minute, hour into hour. It was the fifth day that Terrance texted. "hey, baby—sorry, try again???" Jake couldn't pack his garbage bags fast enough.

Since he'd been back, Terrance had been getting a little rough in bed. He'd slapped him a few times, even left some bruises. Last night, Terrance pushed Jake's face into the pillows so hard, he couldn't breathe. When it was all over, Jake sat up gasping, struggling to fill his lungs with air, his throat pierced by shards of invisible glass. Terrance got up from the bed. "Don't be such a little bitch," he said over his shoulder, heading to the bathroom. "We were just having some fun." But it was all worth it. Terrance is charming, funny, and a successful financial advisor who makes good money. Jake did love him.

"Hello?"

Jake looks up to see Mr. Paul in front of him again.

"I am looking for someplace to eat dinner. Do you have any recommendations?"

Jake nods and leans forward. "Not here," he confides. "Just drinks – and too pricey for too little. If you're up to it, I'd head out." Jake gives him the name of two places within walking distance. "The sidewalks should be pretty clear, but be careful of the ice," he adds. Mr. Paul stares at him a beat too long. Jake notices a few grey strands weave through the gloss of the man's black hair, and a small mole nestles just below his left ear. Mr. Paul leans forward and pushes his extra room key back across the counter.

"In case you need to check on me later," Mr. Paul says. His long fingers rest on the key. They are the color of cinnamon, and for a moment, Jake wants to put one of these fingers in his mouth to see if he can taste the warm spice. He feels a slight sheen of sweat begin to form on his forehead. Mr. Paul smiles slightly, slides his hand back in his pocket, bows his head, and leaves. The door closes behind him.

"Third shift is in the house," Shayla announces, bumping her hip into Jake and setting her McDonalds bag behind the front desk. She unwinds her scarf, pulls off her mittens. "Cold as hell out there. Stay warm, man."

Jake grabs his hat and coat, giving her a quick fist bump on the way out. He exits through the side door and pauses, looking down the street. The Lode Theater's blank marquee juts out like a crooked tooth against the shuttered buildings, and the half-melted snowbanks, grey with road salt, line the nearly empty road. He can see yellow lights from the Downtowner bar glitter over the icy sidewalk a few blocks away. That's where his truck is parked. He should walk over, scrape the ice off the windshield, check the chains on the tires, and head to Terrance's place.

He turns, slides his key back into the side door of the hotel and makes his way up the elevator. He walks down the hallway, the soft lights playing off the silver tinted wallpaper and grey plush carpet. He swipes the key to room 315 and enters.

Inside the closet, a dark suit and two white dress shirts hang neatly from the rack. A pair of black dress shoes point towards the wall, and the small suitcase is tucked in the corner. He turns towards the bed. On the nightstand are a pair of cufflinks and a large Rolex. Jake picks up the watch, feeling its weight in his hand. It is beautiful. The gold band shines, refracting in the light, and the smooth face clicks the time, vibrating slightly under his fingers. He imagines the watch on Mr. Paul's delicate wrist and remembers his eyes, black and clear, seemingly bottomless, as he looked directly at Jake: assessing his worth. Jake turns the watch face down. He pauses. He raises the watch and smashes it against the wall—once, twice, three times. He hears the crack of the glass as it splinters. Small bright shards land near his feet.

Jake turns the watch over. The glass face is completely shattered, the hands frozen. He gently places the watch back on the nightstand. He slides the room key underneath it. He puts his hands in his pockets, bows his head, and leaves, closing the door softly on his way out.

Acknowledgements

I have been fortunate to have several gifted writers who have supported me in learning about the wild and wonderful world of fiction. A special thanks goes to Des Cooper and Katey Schultz, who have provided such thoughtful and patient guidance throughout two years of Monthly Mentorship; John Mauk, whose astute editorial comments and smart observations shaped this collection; Patty Ann McNair, whose writing prompts were the impetus for many of these stories; Anne-Marie Oomen, whose writing class I took at the Interlochen Writers Retreat ten years ago and since then has been a constant north star in my writing life; and Judy Green, my first English teacher and my mother, who (like most mothers) deeply believed in the talents of her child, no matter how deeply hidden they may have been.

Of course, a huge thank you goes to Bruce L. Makie, Brian Gurley, and the judges for the Michigan Writers Chapbook contest. I am so grateful for the work you do. And to my friends: Chris Giroux, Wendy Gronbeck, Elaine Hunyadi, Nancy Nolan, and Melissa Seitz who read (and re-read) multiple drafts of these stories as they unfolded on the page. I owe you many beers and much credit.

And finally, a special thank you to my family: my husband, Steve Klotz; our children, Gaia and Gabe; and our grandchildren, Evelyn, Amelia, Emerson, and Romulus. These folks are some of the very best people I know, and their presence in my life makes all things possible.

About the Fiction Judge

Bryan Gruley is a former journalist and award-winning novelist. He worked for 16 years at *The Wall Street Journal,* including seven as Chicago Bureau Chief. At the *Journal,* he helped cover the September 11 World Trade Center attack and shared in the staff's Pulitzer Prize for that work. His sixth novel, *Bitterfrost,* was published in April, 2025.

About the Author

Helen Raica-Klotz has a Masters in English from Central Michigan University, and she teaches composition courses at Saginaw Valley State University. She's also taught writing at a regional prison, a homeless shelter, an alternative high school, and other places where she can find people with stories to tell. Her fiction and creative non-fiction has appeared in various publications, including *The MacGuffin, Porcupine Literary, Dunes Review, Literary Mama,* and *Great Lakes Review.* Helen lives in northern Michigan with her husband, Steve, and their large black lab, Atticus. Here, she spends much of her time walking through the woods – and avoiding grading papers and cooking.

About Michigan Writers Cooperative Press

This book was published in the spring of 2025 in a signed edition of 100 copies.

This chapbook is part of the Cooperative Series of the Michigan Writers Small Press Project, which was launched in 2005 to give members of Michigan Writers, Inc. a new avenue to publication. All of the chapbooks in this series are an author's first book in that genre. The Cooperative Press shoulders the publishing costs for the first edition, and writers share the marketing and promotional responsibilities in return for the prestige of being published by a press that prints only carefully selected manuscripts.

Chapbook length manuscripts of poetry, short stories, and essays are solicited each year from members and adjudicated by a panel of experienced writers and a judge who is a specialist in a particular genre. For more information, please visit www.michwriters.org.

MICHIGAN WRITERS is an open-membership organization dedicated to providing opportunities for networking, professional growth, and publication for writers of all ages and skill levels in the state of Michigan and beyond.

MANAGING EDITOR: Bruce L. Makie

BOOK DESIGN: Amy Hansen

Other Titles Available
from Michigan Writers Cooperative Press

The Grace of the Eye by Michael Callaghan
Trouble With Faces by Trinna Frever
Box of Echoes by Todd Mercer
Beyond the Reach of Imagination by Duncan Spratt Moran
The Grass Impossibly by Holly Wren Spaulding
The Chocolatier Speaks of his Wife by Catherine Turnbull
Dangerous Exuberance by Leigh Fairey
Point of Sand by Jaimien Delp
Hard Winter, First Thaw by Jenny Robertson
Friday Nights the Whole Town Goes to the Basketball Game
      by Teresa J. Scollon
Seasons for Growing by Sarah Baughman
Forking the Swift by Jennifer Sperry Steinorth
The Rest of Us by John Mauk
Kisses for Laura by Joan Schmeichel
Eat the Apple by Denise Baker
First Risings by Michael Hughes
Fathers and Sons by Bruce L. Makie
Exit Wounds by Jim Crockett
The Solid Living World by Ellen Stone
Bitter Dagaa by Robb Astor
Crime Story by Kris Kuntz
Michaela by Gabriella Burman
Supposing She Dreamed This by Gail Wallace Bozzano
Line and Hook by Kevin Griffin
And Sarah His Wife by Christina Diane Campbell
Proud Flesh by Nancy Parshall
Angel Rides a Bike by Margaret Fedder
Ink by Kathleen Pfeiffer
What Will You Teach Her? by Megan Klco Kellner
Bluetongue and Other Michigan Stories by Ryan Shek
The Mountain Ash by Kathleen Rabbers
This Blue Earth by Sharon Bippus
Upstairs, Listening by Melinda LePere
Twinkies by Kathleen Quigley
The Sound a Car Door Makes by Natalie Tomlin
Brain Aura Blues by Melissa Seitz
Bones and Breath by Ruth Zwald

Michigan
WRITERS

www.ingramcontent.com/pod-product-compliance
Lightning Source LLC
LaVergne TN
LVHW092254310725
817639LV00007B/230